Mommy is the Mayor

Written by Letitia Clark   Illustrated by Sarah K. Turner

alo
PUBLISHING
INTERNATIONAL

ISBN: 978-1-63765-131-5
LCCN: 2021910049

Halo Publishing International, LLC
www.halopublishing.com

Printed and bound in the United States of America

To my children.
Mommy works to make you proud.

Mommy is the mayor. I'm not quite sure what that means.

I just know she's in meetings and takes notes in between.

Mommy has a big office down at city hall.

She even has her picture placed high up on the wall.

Around town some people wave, and some people stare.

But most people just walk by, smile and say, "Hi, Mayor!"

During the elections, we got to do things that were fun.
We walked around neighborhoods, shaking hands, one by one.

We gave out flyers with a picture of our family.
I liked how each one of us smiled so happily.

When neighbors opened the door, they were surprised to see
who was walking with Mommy—my brother and me!

My mommy talked about why she so loved our city
and what our community needed to make it pretty.

She said I was an important member of the team.
And after a long day, we would always get ice cream.

On election night, my parents were glued to the phone—
lots of activity and visitors, some well-known.

Results started coming in, it was all initial.
But then, Mommy was announced: elected official!

The swearing-in ceremony was a big party.
People asked me questions; I felt like such a smarty.

Mommy made an oath, a promise, with a raised right hand.
On behalf of the community, she'd proudly stand.

"Now it's time to get to work and roll up my sleeves.
Be the best mayor I can be; do what I believe."

I was so proud of Mommy. She accomplished her dream,
working hard every day, earning respect and esteem.

When I asked Mommy, "What does a mayor even do?"
She seemed a bit surprised, but said, "Well, let me show you!"

We jumped in the car, and I was excited to go
see the things Mommy does to help the city flow.

"See the crosswalk and stop sign over there by the tree?
The Public Works team and I work for your safety."

Mommy said, "Look to the left. Tell me what you see."
"Oh! I see all my favorite stores—one, two, three."

Mommy had to work with those businesses to prepare
applications and presentations, all to be shared
with city staff on why they deserved to be there.
Mommy said, "There are no details to be spared."

We stopped at the park and continued to talk.
We played on the playground, sat on benches and walked.

"Look around, from all the trees to litter removal,
I had a hand in planning up until approval."

"Wow! You showed me lots of things a mayor can do.
Mommy, I learned many things that I never knew.
Can you tell me more facts? Please, just a few?"

Mommy said, "The sun will soon set, and it will be dark.
But do you know why we can see so well in the park?"

"Because there are lights, high in the sky, low to the ground.
I see small lights and large lights. There are lights all around!"

Mommy smiled and said, "I helped with that project too.
Lighting of many kinds installed by a city crew."

"Lighting helps keep our streets, parks and people safe at night.
Lighting helps those walking or riding maintain good sight."

Before we headed back home, we noticed a big crowd.
Police and firefighters, sirens that were loud.

"I wonder what happened. I hope everything is okay."
Mommy said, "First responders keep accidents at bay."

"By the way," she said, "I help with emergencies, too!
I support our brave men and women in red and blue."

What a fun day! I saw the city through Mommy's eyes.

A mayor must be thoughtful, responsible and wise.

My mommy helps the city be the best it can be.

A mayor is more than meetings and calls, I now see.

It takes much time and attention to details with care,
doing the right thing for others, what is just and fair.

When I'm asked what I learned today, it's knowledge I'll share
about the city, the job and...my mommy the mayor.

23

CPSIA information can be obtained
at www.ICGtesting.com
Printed in the USA
LVHW070924021121
702218LV00002B/19